CARTOON NETWORK.
SCOOBY-DOO!
ADVENTURES

SCOOBY-DOO AND THE PHANTOM COWBOY

SCOOBY-DOO AND THE LEGEND OF THE VAMPIRE

SCOOBY-DOO AND THE WITCH'S GHOST

SCOOBY-DOO ON ZOMBIE ISLAND

Scooby-Doo and the Phantom Cowboy, ISBN 0-439-36586-4, Copyright © 2002 by Hanna-Barbera. Designed by Louise Bova.
Scooby-Doo and the Legend of the Vampire, ISBN 0-439-45522-7, Copyright © 2003 by Hanna-Barbera. Interior design by Bethany Dixon.
Scooby-Doo and the Witch's Ghost, ISBN 0-439-08786-4, Copyright © 1999 by Hanna-Barbera. Design by Peter Koblish.
Scooby-Doo on Zombie Island, ISBN 0-590-38652-2, Copyright © 1998 by Hanna-Barbera. Designed by Joan Ferrigno.

Special thanks to Duendes del Sur for cover and interior illustrations.

(s05)

12 11 10 9 8 7 6 5 4   8 9 10 11/0
Printed in the U.S.A.   24
This edition created exclusively for Barnes & Noble, Inc.
2008 Barnes & Noble Books
ISBN: 0-7607-9542-8
ISBN 13: 978-0-7607-9542-2
This edition printing, August 2008

SCHOLASTIC INC.

New York   Toronto   London   Auckland   Sydney
Mexico City   New Delhi   Hong Kong   Buenos Aires

CARTOON NETWORK

SCOOBY-DOO! and the PHANTOM COWBOY

by Jesse Leon McCann

FOR JAMES MARTIN, A RED-HEADED FAN, HIS PARENTS' JOY

"*Yee-haw!*" Shaggy cheered, waving his cowboy hat around. "I'm, like, an old cowhand from the Rio Grande, y'all!"

"Ree-raw!" Scooby-Doo joined in, spinning his lasso.

Scooby and his friends from Mystery, Inc., were headed to Phantom Gulch, a real-life western ghost town that had been turned into a theme park.

But when the gang got to Phantom Gulch, they got a big surprise — it was completely deserted. It really *was* a ghost town!

WELCOME TO PHANTOM GULCH

CLOSED FOR GOOD!

THE MYSTERY MACHINE

"Jeepers!" Daphne exclaimed. "Where is everybody?"

The gang didn't have to search for long. The remaining citizens of Phantom Gulch were hiding behind the general store. They were about to leave town for good.

"Sorry, folks!" said the town's sheriff, Matt Taff. "Some kind of an ornery ghost has been chasing everyone out of Phantom Gulch. He won't leave us be!"

"That Phantom Cowboy is one mean feller!" Gertie, the owner of the saloon, said, scowling. "And if you know what's good for you, you'll skeedaddle, too!"

"G-g-ghost?" gulped Shaggy.

"Rhantom Rowboy? Roh, ro!" Scooby didn't like the sound of that!

"The Phantom Cowboy has been bothering us for a couple months. We had the worst haunting a few days ago, I reckon," explained Sheriff Matt.

Sheriff Matt said that the creepy cowpoke rode atop a wild, snorting, ghost buffalo! He screamed like a crazy prairie coyote during a full moon. The visitors were so scared, they all left in a hurry and no one had come back since.

"You can't have a tourist attraction without tourists," Sheriff Matt said sadly. "The owners of the town had to close down Phantom Gulch and sell the land to the rancher next door. Now we're all out of work, thanks to that spooky sidewinder!"

"Come on, gang! Let's see if we can get to the bottom of this mystery," Fred suggested.

It wasn't long before they spotted a man who owned the ranch right next door to Phantom Gulch. His name was Harry Parker and he was busy trying to train one of his horses.

"Shucks, kids, them ghosts are mighty fearsome creatures. If I was you, I'd vamoose before they come back again," Mr. Parker exclaimed. "They're always spooking my horses!"

Fred, Shaggy, and Scooby tried to make friends with Mr. Parker's horse. But it snorted and made like it was going to clobber them with its hooves.

"Zoinks! That horse is spooking me!" Shaggy cried.

Despite Mr. Parker's advice, the kids wanted to investigate Phantom Gulch. While the girls went to the courthouse to look for clues, the boys decided to check out the saloon. But on the way there, Scooby spotted something that really scared him.

"Roast racks!" Scooby gulped, grabbed Shaggy, and pointed nervously. "Roast racks! Roast racks!"

"Like, racks of roasts, Scooby?" Shaggy laughed. "Sounds delicious! Where?"

Fred frowned. "Not racks of roasts, Shaggy. *Ghost tracks!*"

"*Zoinks!*" Shaggy exclaimed.

Meanwhile, the girls had found something interesting in the courthouse. After rummaging through an old rolltop desk, they discovered the deed to Phantom Gulch.

"That's strange. According to this, Mr. Parker bought the town last week and sold it to Mega Co. Industries yesterday," Velma said. "Now, why would he do that?"

"*Hmm.* Good question," Daphne answered. "Let's go ask him." Daphne tried to open the door, but it wouldn't budge. "Jeepers! It's locked!"

Just then, they heard the shuffle of feet on the other side of the door. Then came a low, ominous laugh. Someone . . . or some *thing* . . . had them trapped inside!

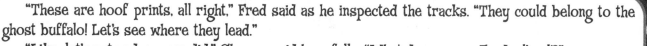

"These are hoof prints, all right," Fred said as he inspected the tracks. "They could belong to the ghost buffalo! Let's see where they lead."

"Like, let's not and say we did," Shaggy said hopefully. "What do you say, Fred, ol' pal?"

"Reah, Red, ol' ral?" Scooby echoed.

Oddly enough, the tracks led right into the saloon. Once they saw there weren't any ghosts there, Shaggy and Scooby thought it was pretty cool to be in a real-life, old west saloon!

"Barkeep!" Shaggy joshed. "We're two tough, ornery hombres! Give us a couple of tall root beers, pardner!"

"Ree-hee-hee-hee!" Scooby giggled.

"Shaggy, stop goofing around and take a look upstairs," Fred said, grinning good-naturedly. "Maybe somebody left a clue in one of the boarding rooms."

"Well, shore thing, feller!" Shaggy lifted the brim of his hat just like a real cowboy. Then he swaggered up the stairs to the second level. "Glad t' oblige y'all, tenderfoot!"

Suddenly, the Phantom Cowboy came charging down the staircase riding his rip-snorting buffalo!

"*Zoinks!* It's the g-g-ghosts! Run!" Shaggy cried. He ran as fast as he could. Meanwhile, the Phantom Cowboy spun a lasso over his head. He was trying to rope Shaggy in!

Shaggy ran down the stairs, across the saloon floor, and out through the double swinging doors. The fearsome ghouls followed close behind!

"Run, Raggy, run!" Scooby hollered.

Daphne and Velma listened at the door till they heard the mysterious footsteps walk away. Then they knew they had to escape from the courthouse so they could warn the boys.

Together, the two girls pushed the rolltop desk under a window. Then Daphne climbed on top and up through the window. Velma clambered up after her.

"It's going to be dark soon," Velma said as they crawled out through the window. "I want to find the guys before the sun sets."

Just then, the ghostly cowboy rode by on his buffalo. "Yaaaaaah!" he cried, spurring his creepy creature onward. "Grrrrrowwwl!!"

"Like, heeeelp!" Shaggy was being pulled behind the buffalo, and it looked like a bumpy ride.

"Jinkies!" cried Velma.

Fred and Scooby-Doo were chasing behind the Phantom Cowboy and his buffalo, trying to rescue Shaggy. The buffalo was fast, however. Just as they were turning a corner and about to disappear from sight, the cowboy turned and pointed at the rest of the gang. "Leave here now!" he called in a booming, eerie voice. "Or I'll come back and get y'all!"

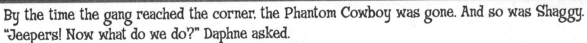

By the time the gang reached the corner, the Phantom Cowboy was gone. And so was Shaggy.

"Jeepers! Now what do we do?" Daphne asked.

"Well, it's getting dark," Velma said. "We can't very well look for Shaggy without some sort of light."

"I'll bet there are some lanterns in there." Fred pointed to an old blacksmith's barn down the street. "Let's take a look."

Sure enough, they found a pair of lanterns and soon had them glowing brightly.

Scooby was feeling very down. His best buddy in the whole world had been whisked away by a spooky desperado riding a buffalo. Velma tried to cheer him with Scooby Snacks, but for once Scooby wasn't in the mood.

"Don't worry, Scooby." Daphne patted him on the head. "Now that we've got light, we're sure to find Shaggy."

Scooby looked determined. "Right!" he barked, jumping to his feet. Soon he was hot on the trail of his kidnapped buddy.

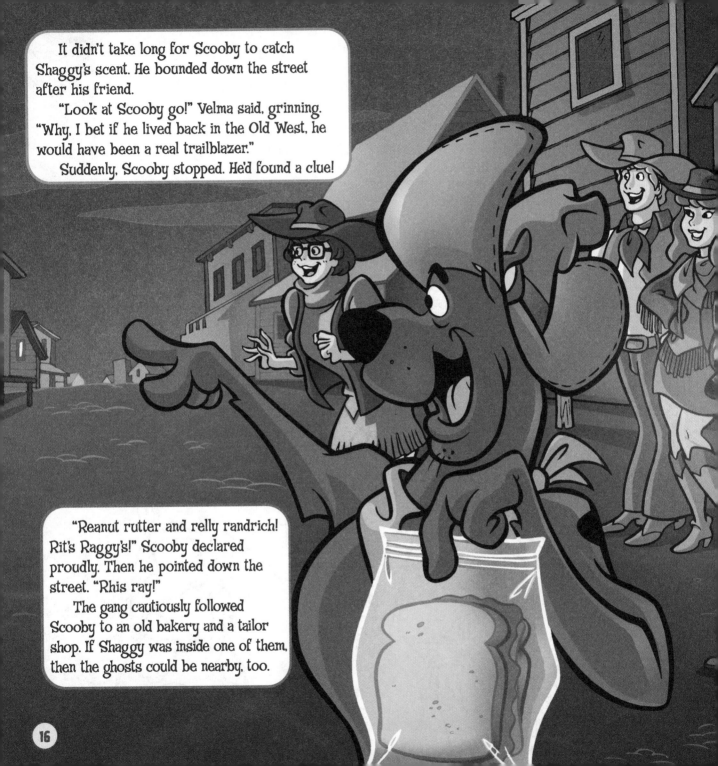

It didn't take long for Scooby to catch Shaggy's scent. He bounded down the street after his friend.

"Look at Scooby go!" Velma said, grinning. "Why, I bet if he lived back in the Old West, he would have been a real trailblazer."

Suddenly, Scooby stopped. He'd found a clue!

"Reanut rutter and relly randrich! Rit's Raggy's!" Scooby declared proudly. Then he pointed down the street. "Rhis ray!"

The gang cautiously followed Scooby to an old bakery and a tailor shop. If Shaggy was inside one of them, then the ghosts could be nearby, too.

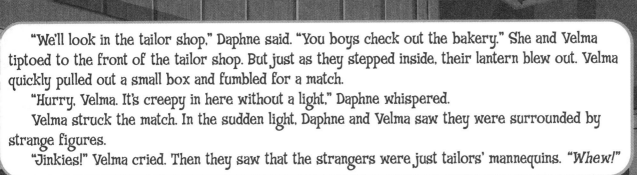

"We'll look in the tailor shop," Daphne said. "You boys check out the bakery." She and Velma tiptoed to the front of the tailor shop. But just as they stepped inside, their lantern blew out. Velma quickly pulled out a small box and fumbled for a match.

"Hurry, Velma. It's creepy in here without a light," Daphne whispered.

Velma struck the match. In the sudden light, Daphne and Velma saw they were surrounded by strange figures.

"Jinkies!" Velma cried. Then they saw that the strangers were just tailors' mannequins. *"Whew!"*

At the same time, Scooby-Doo and Fred were searching the bakery for any sign of Shaggy. Fred checked the back room while Scooby sniffed the floor near the oven. All the flour and baking powder made him let out a big sneeze.

Just as Scooby sneezed, a big flour sack in the corner jumped. Frowning, Scooby tiptoed to the sack of flour. He sniffed at it. Then he poked at it with his paw. Nervously, Scooby untied the top.

"Zoinks!" cried Shaggy, leaping out, all covered in flour. "Don't hurt me, Mr. Phantom Cowboy, sir!"

Scooby's hair stood on end. "Roh, ro! Raggy's a rhost!"

After much yelling and jumping, Scooby realized it was really his friend, not a ghost. They were so happy, they hugged and danced around, getting flour dust everywhere.

"All right, you two," Daphne said, pointing to a nearby water trough. "Time to clean up."

Scooby and Shaggy happily agreed. Then they ran back into the bakery. There were leftover cakes, pies, and other goodies in there.

"Man, like, there's nothing like some good eats after you've had the wits scared out of you!" Shaggy declared, chomping on a bagel.

"Roo raid rit!" agreed Scooby between bites of cake.

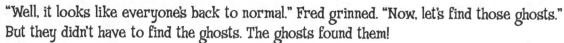

"Well, it looks like everyone's back to normal." Fred grinned. "Now, let's find those ghosts."

But they didn't have to find the ghosts. The ghosts found them!

Out of the darkness emerged the scary rider on his fearsome buffalo. The kids barely dodged out of the way before the ghosts thundered past. Then the cowboy turned his mount around and headed back for another charge. The gang ran for it.

"Ha ha ha ha ha!" cackled the cowboy as he rode down the main street of Phantom Gulch. "I'll give y'all one more chance to leave this place! Now go!"

Then the ghosts disappeared again.

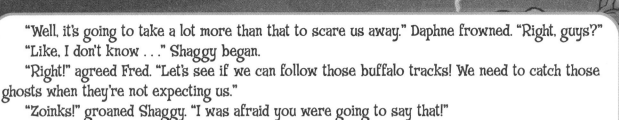

"Well, it's going to take a lot more than that to scare us away." Daphne frowned. "Right, guys?"

"Like, I don't know . . ." Shaggy began.

"Right!" agreed Fred. "Let's see if we can follow those buffalo tracks! We need to catch those ghosts when they're not expecting us."

"Zoinks!" groaned Shaggy. "I was afraid you were going to say that!"

Scooby nodded miserably, "Ree, roo!"

The buffalo tracks led the kids out of town and down a dusty road. After a while, they spotted a campfire burning on a hill. When they got close enough to get a good view, they realized the campfire wasn't on a hill—it was built inside a hill!

AUTHENTIC NATIVE AMERICAN PUEBLO

"Man, what a crazy apartment!" Shaggy said.

"That's a pueblo, Shaggy," Velma explained. "Certain Native American tribes used to build pueblos to live in long ago."

"It looks like our ghost friends have moved in," Fred said. "Let's see if they're up for some company."

Long ladders were leaning against the side of the pueblo, so the gang had an easy time climbing up. Fred peeked into the apartment. No one was in sight. He motioned the others forward.

When they were all inside, the gang spread out, searching for clues. Velma found an old mural painted by elders of the tribe that had once lived there.

"This is fascinating," Velma told the gang. "This mural tells of the coming of the settlers and the extinction of the buffalo. According to legend, a mighty phantom will rise up with his ghostly buffalo and curse the descendants of the settlers forever!"

"But if this cowboy is a ghost, why does he need a campfire at night?" Fred pondered. "Something doesn't add up."

"Like, who cares?" Shaggy was hugging Scooby tightly. "Now that we know the Phantom Cowboy and his creepy critter are the curse-ers, let's fly this coop before we become the curse-ees!"

"Reah! Reah!" Scooby nodded.

"Too late!" bellowed a booming voice. The ghoulish cowboy and his stamping, snorting buffalo sidekick appeared out of nowhere.

As quick as a wink, the gang scrambled back down the ladders to the bottom of the pueblo. They thought that they'd lost the ghostly duo. But all of a sudden, the ghouls appeared from behind a huge boulder and the chase was on again!

Back through the desert the cowboy chased them. Back through the town of Phantom Gulch he rode after them, laughing, whooping, and hollering all the while.

In fact, the ghosts didn't let up until they'd chased the kids all the way back to the Mystery Machine. When he thought he had finally scared the gang away, the cowboy reared up on his buffalo and rode off in a cloud of dust.

But Fred and the girls weren't about to give up so easily.

"There's got to be a logical explanation for this Phantom Cowboy mystery!" Velma exclaimed.

"The only way we'll get to the bottom of this is by catching that ghost, and I've got an idea how," Fred declared. He looked at Shaggy and Scooby. "Of course, we'll need some bait."

"Like, no way, Fred!" Shaggy cried. "I've had my fill of creepy cowboy curses for one night!"

"Right!" Scooby stuck out his tongue. "Bleah! Reepy cowboy rurses!"

After several minutes of wrangling for Scooby Snacks, Shaggy and Scooby agreed to help catch the ghosts. Velma and Daphne took them back to the tailor shop and dressed them like Old West lawmen.

While Fred and the girls went to set up the trap, Shaggy and Scooby went looking for the Phantom Cowboy and his buffalo. The two ghosts had set up a camp in the desert right outside of town. Taking deep breaths for courage, Shaggy and Scooby moseyed right up to the campfire.

"Howdy, Deputy Scoobert! Do y'all see what I see?" Shaggy said in his best cowboy voice. "A coupla mangy varmints having a weenie-roast without a campfire permit!"

"I think we should run these rascals into the pokey!" Shaggy continued. "Wouldn't y'all agree, Deputy Scoobert?"

"Right, Rarshal Raggy," Scooby answered.

The Phantom Cowboy and his ghost buffalo looked at them in surprise for a minute. Then looks of anger came over their faces. They growled and howled at Shaggy and Scooby.

"Like, on the other hand, maybe we should just let them go with a warning this time," Shaggy called as he turned and bolted away. "Run, Scooby-Doo!"

"Roh-oh-oh!" Scooby cried as he raced away from the campfire.

Scooby-Doo and Shaggy fled through the desert, over brambles and around big boulders. They tried hiding behind cacti and running with the tumbleweeds. But no matter what they did, the Phantom Cowboy and his ghostly buffalo stayed right on their heels.

Finally, with no other choice left, the two friends started climbing a small hill nearby. But it was no use — the ghosts stayed right with them. And Scooby and Shaggy were quickly running out of steam!

When Scooby and Shaggy reached the top of the slope, they realized the hill suddenly ended with a sharp dropoff. They were trapped!

"Oh, no!" Shaggy cried.

This made the Phantom Cowboy laugh with evil delight. "I told y'all to vamoose from these here parts." The ghost grinned. "Now it's too late for you!"

"Like, this is it, old pal," Shaggy said to Scooby. "Happy trails!"

"Ro long, Raggy!" Tears came to Scooby's eyes. "Roh, roo hoo hoo!"

But just as the Phantom Cowboy and the ghost buffalo were about to nab Shaggy and Scooby, the villains fell through a hole in the ground. It was a trap—a hole that Fred, Daphne, and Velma had camouflaged with weeds and grass. The hole was carved into the roof of the pueblo to let the smoke from campfires drift out.

Daphne, Fred, and Velma were waiting underneath the hole with a big net, ready to catch the villains. The Phantom Cowboy and the ghost buffalo dropped right into it, as pretty as you please!

"Now, let's see who was behind this mystery." Fred pulled the mask off the captured Phantom Cowboy.

It was Mr. Parker! He had been pretending to be the Phantom Cowboy all along. The ghost buffalo had actually been his ornery horse in disguise.

"Mr. Parker scared away all the people in Phantom Gulch so he could buy the property real cheap," Velma explained as state troopers arrived to take Mr. Parker away. "Then he sold the town for a huge profit to a big company that wanted to build an even bigger western amusement park."

"I would've gotten away with it, too, if it weren't for you meddlin' kids and your dad-burned dog!" sneered Parker.

"Once the judge finds out what Parker did, the town will revert back to its rightful owners," Daphne said, smiling.

Not too long after that, the townspeople who worked at Phantom Gulch returned to their old jobs. Soon visitors started coming back and the town was a lively, old western tourist attraction again.

"We can't thank you enough for solving the mystery and saving Phantom Gulch!" said Sheriff Matt gratefully. "You kids are real western heroes!"

"Like, shucks, Sheriff . . . 't'weren't nothin' any real western heroes couldn't have done," Shaggy drawled. "As long as they had a pardner like Scooby-Doo!"

"Scooby-Dooby-Doo!" cheered Scooby.

SCOOBY-DOO!™
And The
LEGEND OF THE
VAMPIRE
Adapted by Jesse Leon McCann
from the script by Mark E. Turosz

Scooby-Doo and his pals from Mystery, Inc. were on vacation down under! Fred drove the Mystery Machine into the wilds of the Australian Outback. The kids were heading to a music festival at the legendary Vampire Rock.

"*Wow!*" Shaggy exclaimed when he first saw Vampire Rock — it looked scary!

Velma consulted her computer. "The locals call it Vampire Rock because they believe the Yowie Yahoo, an ancient Australian vampire, lives in the rock's caves."

The gang went in search of the music festival, which was located some-where in the woods near Vampire Rock. It didn't take long for Scooby to spot something spooky — a pair of red eyes, watching them from some bushes. Soon Shaggy saw it, too.

"Zoinks! It's the Yowie Yahoo!" Shaggy and Scooby ran and hid behind a big boulder.

"Come on, you two," Velma said, smiling. "I already told you, there's no such thing as vampires."

Scooby and Shaggy wished they could believe her. But if it wasn't true, what had they seen?

Just then, everyone heard a loud growl.

A pack of snarling dingoes — wild Australian dogs — appeared on the rocks above them. Then, as quickly as they came, the dingoes disappeared.

"Hey! Do you guys hear that?" Daphne could hear music now that the dingoes weren't howling.

"Come on, gang!" Fred led them along. "There must be somebody else around here."

The gang headed in the direction of the music. Soon they found themselves at the main stage of the Vampire Rock Music Festival. The stage was
lit up with strobes, projections, and spotlights. More important, some old
friends were onstage, practicing a song.

"Hey! It's the Hex Girls!" Daphne laughed and started dancing to the music.

Shaggy ran up to the stage. "Like, I knew those tunes sounded familiar!"

When the Hex Girls realized they had an audience, they stopped playing
and squinted in the bright lights.

The lead singer, Thorn, grinned. "It *is* you! I thought the lights were getting to me."

It was a nice surprise that the Hex Girls — Thorn, Dusk, and Luna — were going to play at the music festival. They were the opening act. When Velma found out the girls had been there a few days, she asked if they'd seen anything strange since their arrival.

"Like what?" asked Thorn.

Shaggy answered, "Like, how about a big, creepy, scary . . ."

But before Shaggy could finish the question, they were interrupted by Russell and Daniel, the two guys who ran the music festival. They were worried because the Hex Girls' music had suddenly stopped.

"The finalists in our band contest keep disappearing," Russell explained sadly.

"Now more bands are quitting because another singer was kidnapped today," Daniel added.

Shaggy's eyes opened wide. "Like, maybe they were kidnapped by big, creepy, scary . . ."

A shaky voice finished his sentence. "Vampires!"

The voice belonged to a strange old man in a jeep, who started driving away. "I warned you terrible things would happen, Daniel!"

"That was my grandfather, Malcolm," Daniel explained. "He doesn't think we should have a music festival because of the Yowie Yahoo."

Daniel and Russell explained that the Yowie Yahoo had kidnapped a band called Wildwind, who had lost the previous year's contest. The Yowie Yahoo made Wildwind into his vampires, and they were terrorizing this year's bands.

"The best way to solve this mystery is to go undercover as a rock band," Fred declared. "If we're lucky, the Wildwind vampires will try to kidnap us next."

"Like, I don't want to be that lucky!" Shaggy said.

"Ruh-uh!" agreed Scooby.

The next day, the gang was onstage, dressed like a rock group. Daphne and Velma found some strange white powder on top of some amplifiers — it was glowing white makeup. Fred discovered a footprint made of a mysterious sticky, gooey substance. These were definitely clues!

Before they could do any more investigating, a golf cart pulled up to the stage. In the cart was the rock group called the Bad Omens. Behind the wheel was their manager, Jasper Ridgeway, who once managed the missing band Wildwind. When the Bad Omens saw Scooby playing the drums, they laughed.

"Why don't you amateurs take a break?" one of them sneered.

After Scooby and the gang left the stage to make way for the Bad Omens, Fred whispered, "I think we may have just met our so-called vampires."

"The Bad Omens?" asked Velma.

"Exactly," said Fred. "Jasper Ridgeway seems like the kind of guy who'd do anything to have his band win the competition."

While Scooby and Shaggy went to check out the concession stands, the others decided to investigate Jasper's plush trailer. As luck would have it, Jasper wasn't there, and they were able to sneak in.

Jasper's trailer was crowded with Wildwind memorabilia.

"There's so much stuff in here, it's going to be hard to tell the clues from the collectibles," said Daphne.

"Jinkies! I think I already found a clue!" Velma pulled a costume from inside a cabinet. "This looks just like what Wildwind used to wear."

They left the trailer, certain that Jasper and the Bad Omens were behind the kidnappings.

Meanwhile, Scooby-Doo and Shaggy were checking out the deserted concession-stand area in the best way possible — by sampling all the food! They were enjoying all sorts of Australian food and drinks laid out on a big table.

"Australians call this 'Damper.'" Shaggy held up a big piece of bread with jam. "But, like, it's not putting a damper on my appetite!"

Shaggy gobbled down the bread, then slurped down a soda. "Like, what's next, old buddy?"

But Scooby wasn't eating. He was diving under the table!

"Rampires," Scooby squeaked and pointed with his tail. The Wildwind vampires had appeared right behind Shaggy!

"Zoinks! Like, now I'm not hungry at all!" Shaggy ducked under the table, too.

Shaggy and Scooby bolted, carrying the table on their backs until they were several feet away. Soon the two buddies were running through the concession-stand area with the angry vampires right behind them!

Scooby and Shaggy ran into a tent that sold Italian food and threw on some uniforms, pretending that they worked there. When a vampire came in, they served him a big plate of spaghetti and meatballs.

The vampire forgot about the chase and looked at the plate of food with delight. Faster than even Shaggy or Scooby could have eaten it, the spaghetti was gone.

The only problem was, the vampire was now eyeing them as if he'd like to eat *them* for dessert! Scooby and Shaggy dashed away again.

Next Shaggy and Scooby fled into a tent called the House of Mirrors. Inside were fun-house mirrors that made their reflections look goofy.

Shaggy and Scooby forgot that they were running from creepy vampires when they saw their silly reflections in the mirrors. They laughed and laughed. That is, until they saw the reflection of one of the Wildwind vampires behind them. Then they cried . . . and ran away again!

Scooby-Doo and Shaggy raced back to the main stage. The Bad Omens were still practicing when Shaggy and Scooby ran through in a panic.

The band didn't know what to think. Then, while Scooby and Shaggy hid, a huge, spinning cloud appeared above the stage. Suddenly, a giant vampire emerged from the top of the swirling cloud. It was the Yowie Yahoo!

"Bwah-hah-hah-hah-hah!" the Yowie Yahoo laughed evilly.

Before the Bad Omens had time to think, the Wildwind vampires flew down and grabbed them. Scooby and Shaggy peeked up just in time to watch them all disappear, leaving the stage in a shambles. All that was left behind was a sweet-smelling smoke in the air.

Moments later, Fred, Daphne, and Velma ran up. Shaggy and Scooby told them what had happened to the Bad Omens.

"Hmmm. Well, there go our prime suspects," Fred said.

Late that night, two motorcycles pulled into the music festival campground, waking everybody up. It was a band called Two Skinny Dudes. Their real names were Barry and Harry. They laughed when Daniel told them he was glad they hadn't been kidnapped by vampires like the other bands.

"If you weren't kidnapped, where have you been?" Fred asked suspiciously.

"Exploring Vampire Rock," answered Barry, showing them his rock-climbing equipment. "We liked it so much, we decided to camp there."

"But we didn't see a single vampire," said Harry.

The next day, the gang went with Daniel to visit his grandfather, Malcolm, who was an expert on the Yowie Yahoo legend.

Malcolm was busy sending smoke signals to other members of his tribe. He used branches from a tree that grew nearby to make a sweet-smelling smoke. The same tree had a very sticky, gooey sap. Scooby found that out the hard way when he got stuck to the tree and disturbed a cranky koala bear.

"The Yowie Yahoo can only be destroyed by sunlight," Malcolm said with a frown. "You should cancel the music festival before the vampires get everyone — including you."

The gang decided the only way to get to the bottom of the mystery was by visiting Vampire Rock themselves. They climbed up a steep path and came to a rickety bridge.

"Jeepers! I knew Vampire Rock was big, but not this big," Daphne said.

As soon as everyone had crossed the bridge, they hit a fork in the path. Fred decided they had better split up.

"Zoinks! Vacation has really brought us closer together," Shaggy said nervously. "Like, it would be a shame to split up now!"

After sending Shaggy and Scooby in one direction, Fred and the girls went in another. It didn't take long for them to discover a hidden passage that led to a secret warehouse.

"Wow!" exclaimed Daphne. "I was expecting a vampire's lair to be more spooky."

There was technical equipment everywhere. It was all stuff used for rock concerts — projectors, wind machines, special-effects units, smoke machines, and sound amplifiers. The gang could tell someone had been there recently, because all the lanterns were lit. But who?

Meanwhile, Scooby and Shaggy explored the other way around Vampire Rock. Suddenly, they heard the sound of growling coming from behind them!

"D-d-dingo dogs!" cried Shaggy.

They backed away from the ferocious, snarling beasts. Unfortunately, their escape was blocked by a wall of rock and a nearby mountain pool.

"We can't run and we can't climb," Shaggy said. "Like, we need a miracle, Scoob!"

Minutes before, Daphne had gotten separated from Fred and Velma. Before long, she ran into one of the creepy vampires. It was hanging upside down from the ceiling, smiling at her.

"Jeepers!" Daphne ran down a dark tunnel that ended with a long drop off a cliff to a pool of water far below.

The vampire was right behind her. Daphne had no choice but to jump! Luckily, the splash she made frightened the dingoes away from Scooby and Shaggy. They were all saved!

"Like I said, a miracle." Shaggy smiled. "Or Daphne doing a cannonball off a cliff!"

Soon the Mystery, Inc. gang was back together again. And the Wildwind vampires were right behind them!

"We need to stay together and remain calm," Fred said, as the gang ran away from the vampires.

Just then, the Yowie Yahoo appeared out of a swirling cloud above them. He let out a thunderous roar! And the Wildwind vampires were flying through the air, swooping down in attack formation!

"Like, if there was ever a time not to be calm, this is it!" cried Shaggy.

The Yowie Yahoo opened his mouth again and giant fireballs shot out. Great blasts of flame scorched the ground all around them. Shaggy and Scooby hid as explosions of rock rained down all around them.

Then the Yowie Yahoo slammed his mighty fists together. The force of his blows shook the earth. He blew a burst of hot air from his mouth. Fred, Velma, and Daphne were almost blown away!

"Like, the Yowie Yahoo sure is full of hot air!" Shaggy cried.

Velma looked toward the east, and then back to the others. "The sun is almost up."

Fred smiled. "Vampires have to get inside, or the sunlight will destroy them."

The Wildwind vampires had disappeared, but the Yowie Yahoo stayed in the shadows of Vampire Rock and continued his attack. He was heading right for Scooby-Doo!

"Relp!" gulped Scooby.

Then an amazing thing happened. Just as it looked like the Yowie Yahoo was sure to get Scooby, a ray of sunlight shone onto Scooby's dog tag. The reflected light bounced off the tag and hit the Yowie Yahoo square in the chest. The giant vampire began to fade, and then it disappeared into thin air!

"Scooby, you did it!" Daphne cheered. "You defeated the Yowie Yahoo!"

Just when everything seemed like it was going to be okay, the Wildwind vampires returned to chase the gang again — in broad daylight! The sun was up and it didn't hurt them at all. The vampires chased the kids all the way back to the music festival grounds.

"Zoinks!" yelled Shaggy. "Didn't these vampires read the rule book?"

Just then, Daniel appeared to set a trap into action. He threw his boomerang and hit a rope, which released a net. They had captured the vampires!

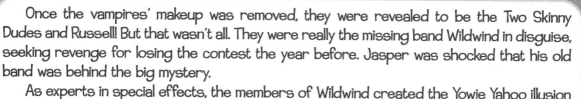

Once the vampires' makeup was removed, they were revealed to be the Two Skinny Dudes and Russell! But that wasn't all. They were really the missing band Wildwind in disguise, seeking revenge for losing the contest the year before. Jasper was shocked that his old band was behind the big mystery.

As experts in special effects, the members of Wildwind created the Yowie Yahoo illusion with a hologram projection — which is why it disappeared when the light from Scooby's tag hit it. They used the same sweet-smelling, sticky-sapped tree branches that Malcolm had used to make all the smoke. And they used their rock-climbing gear to make it appear as if they were flying.

"We would have gotten away with it, if it weren't for you meddling kids!" muttered Russell.

That night, after the concert, Daniel's voice boomed over the speakers. "Now the winners of this year's band contest . . . the Meddling Kids!" The crowd cheered.

The Meddling Kids were a hit! The Hex Girls even joined the gang onstage as backup singers. Everyone had a great time, especially Scooby-Doo, who beat out a groovy rhythm on the drums! "Rooby-dooby-doo!" he cheered.

SCOOBY-DOO!
WITCH'S and the GHOST

Based on the screenplay
"Scooby-Doo and the Witch's Ghost"
by Davis Doi & Glenn Leopold

Adapted by Gail Herman

Story by Rick Copp & David Goodman

Scooby-Doo and his friends were in a museum disguised as exhibits! They were trying to solve a mystery about warrior mummies.

Suddenly the friends spied the mummies. They were about to uncover the culprits behind the mystery — when someone else did it for them!

The mysterious hero?

"Ben Ravencroft!" Velma cried, "the horror writer!"

The famous writer knew the Mystery, Inc. gang, too. Ben told them that he happened to be at the museum doing research for a book. "I've always admired *your* mystery-solving work," he said to Scooby and his friends. Then he added, "I'm going to my hometown of Oakhaven this weekend. It's so peaceful, why don't you come?"

"Reah!" said Scooby.

But Oakhaven wasn't peaceful at all. Traffic snarled the streets and tourists scurried to buy T-shirts at Mr. McKnight's drugstore.

Ben read from a shirt: "I met the ghost of Oakhaven." What was *that* about?

"Ghost?" said Shaggy. "Rhost?" echoed Scooby. Was there really a ghost in Oakhaven?

Just then Mayor Corey hurried over. "That's not just any ghost," he explained to the gang. "That's the ghost of Sarah Ravencroft. She's one of Ben's ancestors. We must have disturbed her spirit when we built our Puritan Village."

The townspeople had built a model village for tourists to visit — one that looked centuries old, with houses, shops, and people dressed in Puritan costumes. Mayor Corey proudly showed everyone the sights — including old-fashioned prison stocks. Shaggy got into the spirit right away. Pretending to be locked up, he cried, "Look, Scoob! I've been caught!"

Scooby grinned, then took a turn with an old butter churn . . . only he didn't stir it to turn milk into butter. He played it like a guitar. Suddenly he dropped the churn.

"Ropher!" cried Scooby, chasing a gopher down a hole. A moment later he popped back up. He had lost the gopher, but found a small rusty buckle.

"Too bad Scooby didn't find Sarah Ravencroft's journal," Ben told the gang. "She was accused of being a witch. That book would clear our family name."

The gang looked around the village. They walked past a turkey pen and a pumpkin patch. Then Shaggy and Scooby strolled over to Oakhaven Restaurant for lunch. The owner, Jack, read them all the items on the menu.

Shaggy's mouth watered. "Sounds great," he said. "Like give us two of everything!"

Meanwhile, at Ben Ravencroft's mansion, Daphne, Fred, and Velma stared wide-eyed at the horror writer's gruesome knickknacks and pictures. Fred wandered over to a portrait — a young Puritan woman, grasping a journal, standing by a tall oak tree. He read the nameplate: "Sarah Ravencroft."

Velma stepped closer. So *this* was the ancestor whose ghost was now haunting the town.

Ben saw Velma staring at the picture. "Sarah was a Wiccan," Ben explained, "a kind of medicine woman, like a doctor."

"I've read about them," Velma said. "Wiccans don't use ordinary medicine. They understand the forces of nature — herbs and plants — and use them for healing."

"Sarah treated her patients under a large oak tree," Ben went on. "I've searched for that tree around town, hoping to find Sarah's journal, which may have been buried there. But I haven't come up with a thing."

A few minutes later, everyone went to meet Shaggy and Scooby. At the Oakhaven Restaurant, shocked customers were watching the friends chow down — it was like nothing they'd ever seen!

Scooby chomped at a giant hambone. Shaggy stuffed handfuls of fries into his mouth. "Is there anything left in the kitchen?" Velma joked, eyeing the plates piled high with bones and leftovers.

"Let's go and see if that ghost makes an appearance tonight," Fred said to Shaggy and Scooby.

The two friends stared, frightened, at each other. "Like we'd love to," Shaggy told his friends. "But we haven't had dessert yet."

So Ben took Velma, Daphne, and Fred around town trying to spot the ghost, while Shaggy and Scooby gobbled down twelve pies. Finally they staggered out of the restaurant. It was nighttime now, and the dark street was empty.

Thud, thud. Suddenly, loud, heavy footsteps sounded. Shabby and Scooby stopped short. Who was coming?

Three shadowy shapes glided over to them.

"Girls!" Shaggy exclaimed, slicking back his hair. "Hi!" The girls paused under a streetlight. They wore dark, somber clothes. Their faces were deathly pale, and their hair was long and straggly. "Hi," the girls replied with wicked grins. Each one had sharp, jagged teeth!

"I thought there was only *one* witch's ghost!" Shaggy panted as he and Scooby raced away.

All at once, a powerful wind whipped down the street. Leaves swirled and trees shook with the force. The witch's ghost appeared! She looked just like Shaggy imagined, with a pointy hat and cackling voice.

"This town ruined me," shrieked the ghost. "And now it will pay!"

She raised one arm. A red-hot fireball shot out from her fingertips.

Scooby and Shaggy took off. The witch's ghost tossed another fireball, and Shaggy leaped into the air. He held onto Scooby as they raced around the corner — careening straight into Velma, Daphne, Fred, and Ben Ravencroft.

"Ritch's rhost!" cried Scooby.

"Witch's ghost!" Velma repeated. "*You* saw her! Where?" Shaggy led everyone back to the spot, babbling about fireballs and three other witches.

Velma switched on a flashlight. "Hmmm," she said, kneeling to examine some powder. "Fireballs . . ."

"Ahhhh!" A wailing sound echoed through town and strange green lights flickered in the distance.

The gang and Ben tracked the sound and lights to a large clearing in the woods. A stage stood at one end, with three figures swaying under a strange green light show. The noise was music!

"Zoinks!" said Shaggy. "It's those other witches!"

"It's just a band," Fred said. He pointed to a sign that said "Hex Girls" behind the girls. "I heard they're putting on a concert tomorrow night. They must be rehearsing."

No longer scared, Shaggy and Scooby danced to the music. The song ended, and the girls introduced themselves as Thorn, Luna, and Dusk. Fred whispered to Velma, "These girls seem suspicious. Daphne and I will keep an eye on them."

Velma wanted to do more exploring, so she led the others to the witch's ghost spot. "Tire tracks!" she exclaimed, shining her flashlight on some marks in the dirt. "Let's see where they lead!"

Everyone followed the tracks to a large barn. "Shh!" said Velma, pulling everyone into the shadows as a man hurried out. It was the mayor!

"Jinkies!" said Velma, surprised. The barn doors were now padlocked shut, so Ben hoisted her up to a window and she climbed inside. A truck stood in the center of the barn. Its engine was still warm. Why would someone drive a construction truck at night? Velma wondered.

Meanwhile, Shaggy and Scooby followed the mayor. They tried to be quiet, but Mayor Corey stopped and whirled around. The street was empty. So he shrugged and walked on. He didn't notice the guys hiding inside a broken mailbox.

A few minutes later, Shaggy and Scooby watched the mayor take a package from a shopkeeper. Then they trailed him to a hotel, where he delivered the package to the owner.

"Zoinks!" Shaggy whispered. "This mayor is one busy guy!"

"Reah!" Scooby agreed.

Shaggy and Scooby continued to follow the mayor around town. But they lost sight of him near an old warehouse.

"Ahhhh!" A loud moan echoed down from the roof, and suddenly the witch's ghost appeared! She swooped toward the guys, reaching out for them with clawed hands.

Scooby and Shaggy tried to run. They spun their legs wildly, but that only made them dig a hole in the dirt. They couldn't get out!

"This town will pay!" the witch's ghost moaned again.

"Send them a bill!" Shaggy yelled back as they finally scrambled free. "But leave *us* alone!"

The guys raced right past their friends and squeezed into another mailbox, quivering with fear. "So what happened?" Velma asked the shaking mailbox.

Shaggy explained everything. Then Fred described a strange ceremony the Hex Girl named Thorn had performed. She had crushed plants and flowers to make some sort of potion.

Velma thought a moment. A phone call would have to be made, and then . . .

"I can solve the mystery," she declared, "and we can leave."

Leave! Shaggy, then Scooby popped free of the mailbox and hugged Velma with joy.

"But I need one more clue," she added.

Back at the concert stage, Velma whispered her plan to the gang. Fred and Daphne nodded, then scurried into the woods. But Shaggy and Scooby were more interested in putting on a show.

"Hey!" Thorn hissed, suddenly appearing behind the pals. She bared her fangs menacingly.

Scooby gulped. "Rorry!"

"Thanks for coming," Velma said, hurrying to greet the spooky musicians.

"But why did you call us?" Thorn asked. "What are we doing here?"

All at once, a blast of wind hit the stage. The witch's ghost was back!

"Runnnnn!" Shaggy cried, his hair standing on end. The ghost hurled a fireball. Everyone scrambled off stage, with the witch's ghost close behind.

It was going just the way Velma had planned. Now to catch the ghost! Suddenly Velma flung herself to the ground, pretending to trip. The ghost screeched to a stop.

"Now!" Velma shouted into the woods.

A tree branch sprang forward, snapping a wire in two. The ghost flew backward out of control — straight into a net hung between two bushes. Velma had set a trap!

Daphne and Fred came out from behind the bushes. Fred looked at the ghost, who was trapped and moaning in the net.

"Let's see who this is," he said. He pulled off the witch mask.

Everyone gasped. "Like, it's the T-shirt guy!" Shaggy exclaimed. "Mr. McKnight!" He was the man who ran the drugstore and, as it turned out, he was also Thorn's father.

"Daddy!" said Thorn.

"I can explain what happened," Velma said. "Mr. McKnight got the fireball powder from Thorn's stage props."

Then she pointed to the truck. It was the same one she'd seen in the barn. Now it was parked in the woods next to a giant fan. "The truck has a wire device that made the ghost fly. The fan created the wind. So it took more than one person to pull off this scam."

Jack the restaurant owner stepped out of the darkness, followed by the hotel owner, the shopkeeper, and finally the mayor. They hung their heads, ashamed.

"These people made money from the tourists who came to see the 'ghost,'" Velma said.

"And *we're* not witches," one Hex Girl told them, taking out her fake fangs. "We just pretend for our act. But Thorn really is a Wiccan. She even makes herbal drinks to soothe our throats for singing."

So *that* was the potion!

"We found Sarah's gravestone when we built our Puritan Village," the mayor went on. "We remembered how she'd been accused of witchcraft. So we used her as our ghost. But we didn't find that journal."

Velma thought back to the portrait in Ben's home. Sarah stood in front of an old oak tree, holding a book that had a buckle. The buckle was just like the one Scooby had found when he chased that gopher down a hole — right by the stump of an oak tree! "And where there's a buckle," Velma told herself, "maybe there's a book!"

Immediately, she dangled two Scooby Snacks in front of Scooby and told him to find the hole. He raced to the spot — and dug up a strange-looking book.

Ben grabbed it. He grinned, but it was an evil grin that darkened his face. "This isn't a journal," he growled in a low, threatening voice. "It's a spellbook. Sarah *was* a witch!"

Velma gasped. He had known it all along!

"And I set up the museum meeting," he told the gang, "so you could help me find it!"

Ben had tricked them all — the gang from Mystery, Inc., the mayor and his friends, the Hex Girls. And now, his evil plans were about to unfold.

"I will summon Sarah," Ben cried. "Together we will rule the world!"

The book glowed red. The wind whipped fiercely, pushing everyone back. The townspeople flew into the stocks of the Puritan Village, and the Hex Girls were tied to a post. Thunder boomed. Lightning flashed. Clouds shifted, and suddenly the witch's ghost — the *real* witch's ghost — swept through the sky.

"Serve me!" Ben commanded.

But the witch's ghost had *other* ideas! "I serve no one!" She glared at Ben, holding out her arm. A fire blast shot out and caught Ben up in a green glowing ball.

The spellbook dropped to the ground. "We need that book," Velma whispered to Shaggy and Scooby.

"Get close to that evil bad guy Ben?" Shaggy groaned. But he and Scooby dashed away while the witch flung fireball after fireball at the others.

"The Wiccans imprisoned me in the book!" Sarah shrieked. "And no one will do that again!"

One blast zapped the pumpkin patch. Boom! The pumpkins exploded and changed into monster creatures, skittering on vine-legs. "Jinkies!" cried Velma, as she sped quickly away.

For a second, the coast was clear, so Shaggy grabbed the book. But the witch's ghost sent one more fireball. It crashed into the turkey pen. "Get them, birds," she ordered.

"Even we're not scared of that," Shaggy said. Only suddenly the turkey grew into a huge monstrous creature. "Like now we are!" said Shaggy.

He and Scooby raced into a museum building, and rushed out in Puritan costumes. Shaggy held a giant turkey baster while Scooby held a bowl of stuffing. "Uh-oh!" squawked the turkey, turning tail to run.

"Thou will not escape!" the witch's ghost cackled. She gripped Scooby by the tail, holding him upside down.

"Zoinks!" cried Shaggy, jumping out of his costume. He flung a bucket of water at the witch's ghost — just like Dorothy had done in *The Wizard of Oz*.

"Hey!" he said, surprised. "Like you're not melting!" He tossed the bucket and it landed on the witch's head. She dropped Scooby. "Raggy, run!" cried Scooby as the bucket popped free.

Shaggy grabbed the witch's spellbook and threw it to Velma. She flipped through the pages, searching for a spell to imprison Sarah.

"Here!" she said to Thorn. "You're a Wiccan. Read it!"

The witch was getting closer! Quickly Thorn read, "Ancient evil get thee hence . . ."

Suddenly the book jumped out of Thorn's hand, glowing and crackling with energy. The wind died away and Sarah's ghost was sucked into its pages. "I won't go back alone!" she cried, grabbing Ben's foot. Whoosh! They disappeared inside the spellbook — together.

That night, the Hex Girls along with Shaggy and Scooby performed their concert to a sell-out crowd. The giant turkey never returned to its regular size, and tourists were still flocking to Oakhaven to see it. The mayor and townspeople grinned happily.

"Scooby-dooby-doo," Scooby hissed and grinned back, showing off his brand-new fangs.

SCOOBY-DOO ON ZOMBIE ISLAND

Based on the screenplay by Glenn Leopold
Story by Glenn Leopold and Davis Doi

Adapted by Gail Herman

HANNA-BARBERA AND WARNER BROS.
PRESENT "SCOOBY-DOO ON ZOMBIE ISLAND"
EXECUTIVE PRODUCER JEAN MacCURDY SUPERVISING PRODUCER DAVIS DOI PRODUCER COS ANZILOTTI
WRITTEN BY GLENN LEOPOLD ASSOCIATE PRODUCER VICTORIA McCOLLUM DIRECTED BY JIM STENSTRUM
BASED UPON CHARACTERS CREATED BY WILLIAM HANNA AND JOSEPH BARBERA

ONLY AVAILABLE ON VIDEO

The gang from Mystery, Inc. was in a dark, eerie castle. They thought they'd caught the slimy moat monster. But then Daphne, Fred, Velma, Shaggy, and Scooby looked closer. Something was wrong!

So they tugged here and there — and off came a mask!

The monster was just an ordinary man in a costume.

"The monsters and ghosts always turned out to be bad guys in masks," Daphne, who was now a reporter, was telling the host of a TV talk show. "It got boring."

That's why the Mystery, Inc. gang split up.

But Daphne hadn't totally given up on finding real ghosts and monsters — yet.

"I'm doing a new series of shows," she told the host. "*Haunted America*. And this time I'm going to find real haunted houses!"

But Daphne was sad. Ghost hunting without her old friends wouldn't be the same. She missed the gang.

Fred, who worked with Daphne, had an idea.

Shaggy and Scooby had new jobs now. They worked at the airport, making sure no one tried to smuggle illegal things into the country. Their favorite find: food!

Shaggy and Scooby took a break to watch Daphne on TV. "Like, we really miss you, too," Shaggy said to Daphne, onscreen.

"Reah," Scooby sniffed.

AIRPORT
CUSTOMS

Then Shaggy and Scooby went back to work. Scooby sniffed through some baggage. He pulled out a big wheel of cheese!

He and Shaggy were hungry. So . . . they ate the cheese.

Later, their boss walked in. He was angry. "You ate the evidence! You're fired!"

Fired? Shaggy and Scooby sobbed.

But just then the phone rang. Things were looking up!

Velma's new job was selling books at Dinkley's Mystery Bookshop. But she was bored. Solving mysteries is a lot more fun than selling them, she told herself.

The phone rang. "Jinkies!" she exclaimed when she heard Fred's voice. "Count me in!"

The next day, Fred drove the Mystery Machine van to Daphne's home. She was ready to start work on *Haunted America*.

Then, Fred flung open the back doors.

"Surprise!" shouted Velma and Shaggy.

"Rurprise!" barked Scooby.

The gang was back together!

They were off to New Orleans, Louisiana — a city with great ghosts, real haunted houses, and yummy food!

Well, at least the food was yummy in New Orleans.

Everything else turned out to be fake.

The "ghost" Fred and Daphne discovered at a séance was really a picture from a movie projector.

The "man-bat" was just a crook trying to keep people out of the cemetery.

Even the "ghost" captain aboard a riverboat turned out to be a woman in a costume.

Daphne was dejected. "I need to find a real ghost for my show," she told the gang. While Shaggy and Scooby searched for a snack, Daphne, Fred, and Velma sat in an outdoor market. Suddenly, a woman came up to them.

She was Lena Dupree. She worked as a chef on nearby Moonscar Island. "It's a place," Lena whispered, "that's haunted by the ghost of the pirate Morgan Moonscar."

Lena invited everyone to visit the island and see for themselves. They had to take a ferryboat to get there.

Jacques, the captain, pointed to the murky water. "People go into that bayou and never come out," he said in a low voice.

Then Lena saw Scooby. "You have a dog!" she interrupted. She wasn't happy.

"Rog?" Scooby repeated. "Rwhere?"

Lena scowled. "My boss, Ms. Simone Lenoir, keeps cats."

"Like, don't worry," Shaggy told her. "Scooby is great with cats."

Soon Moonscar Island loomed in the distance. Fred began to videotape the dense trees, swamps, and hanging moss. It was a perfect place for ghosts. Simone's house seemed perfect, too — a big, grand mansion, crawling with cats.

"Rats!" Scooby said excitedly. He streaked toward them — tearing up the garden!

"Hey, you mutt!" Beau the gardener tried to stop him. But Scooby chased one cat up the stairs — right into the arms of Simone Lenoir. She was *not* amused.

Shaggy took Scooby to the kitchen to keep him busy, while Simone gave the others a tour of the house.

"The island is deserted now," she told the gang, "but a long time ago it was a hot-pepper plantation. Once it served as a Civil War barracks for soldiers. Another time, it was used as a trading post. It was even a pirate hideaway. There were rumors Morgan Moonscar hid treasure on the island."

Suddenly, Simone's story was interrupted by screams echoing through the house.

"The guys!" exclaimed Velma.

Everyone rushed into the kitchen. Scooby pointed a shaking paw at the wall. The words *GET OUT* were carved into the wood.

"Ghost writing!" Shaggy explained.

A cold wind whipped through the room. Fred began to film everything.

All at once, a strange ooze seeped out of the wall! The ooze formed one word. *BEWARE!*

When Fred played back the tape, a ghostly pirate with a moon-shaped scar came into focus.

"It's the ghost of Morgan Moonscar," Simone declared.

"No, it's just a guy in a pirate suit," Fred protested. "He's trying to scare people away from the treasure."

But why did he only show up on tape? Scooby and Shaggy were nervous.

"We're getting some food," Shaggy said. "To go!"

Scooby and Shaggy carried sandwiches and potato salad outside. But before they could eat, the cats ran off with the potato salad.

In a flash, Scooby charged after them . . . through a marshy stream . . . around some logs . . . back to the grounds of the house.

"Stop, Scooby!" Shaggy tried to catch him. And they both stumbled headlong into a deep hole — shaped like a grave!

"Like, hang on, Scoob," Shaggy reassured him. "I'll have us out in a sec."

Shaggy grabbed a root sticking out of the dirt wall and tried to pull himself up.

Rrrrrip! The root tore free.

Shaggy fell on Scooby. Dirt rained down, leaving a big empty space in the wall.

Then, a skeleton hand floated out and the skies darkened. More bones drifted over the grave and, suddenly, the ghostly ooze wrapped them all together to form Morgan Moonscar: zombie!

"Ahh!" wailed the zombie.

"Rahh!" screamed Scooby as a ghostly hand snaked toward him.

Shaggy jumped on Scooby's back, bounced off his head, and out of the grave.

Then, he grabbed Scooby's tail and yanked him out, too. Still screaming, the two bolted for the house — and barreled straight into Beau the gardener.

Hearing the cries, the rest of the gang raced over.

"We saw a zombie!" Shaggy shouted.

Everyone looked at Beau suspiciously. He had been awfully close to the scene.

Hoping for a glimpse of real zombies, Daphne wanted to stay the night. Scooby and Shaggy had already seen enough. They wanted to leave, now!

But when Lena offered to make dinner, Scooby and Shaggy changed their minds. Everyone would stay the night.

Velma, Daphne, and Fred noticed something weird when they went upstairs to unpack. Little bits of their clothing were missing: a part of a tie, a piece of cloth. But they didn't stress. What was the big deal, when there was a zombie ghost?

When they came down to dinner, Simone frowned at Scooby. "The dog will have to eat outside," she said.

That was okay. Shaggy and Scooby would take the van and find a quiet place to chow down.

Later, everyone heard screams and the sounds of the van screeching through the woods. Daphne, Fred, and Velma dashed into the darkness.

"Scooby!" they called. "Shaggy!"

All at once a shadowy figure stepped into their path. Beau!

Velma glared at him. He was right at the scene — again. She was going to keep a close eye on him now.

Deep in the woods, the gang found the van. But Scooby and Shaggy were gone.

Suddenly, a pirate zombie grabbed Daphne. She flipped the creature over her head, and he crashed to the ground.

Then she heard a noise. More zombies! Daphne thought, flipping another body. But this time, it was only Shaggy, who landed — splat! — on the zombie.

"Zoinks!" he cried.

"Take it easy," said Fred. "It's just a mask. I'll show you."

Fred pulled and tugged as hard as he could. The zombie's face stretched, then snapped back into place. Fred gasped.

This zombie was for real!

Shaggy and Scooby bolted away as more zombies rose from the water — Civil War soldiers, pirates, all different kinds. Fred lifted his video camera to film them. But then, he heard Lena screaming back at the house.

Racing to help Lena, Fred accidentally dropped the camera into quicksand. "Oh, no!" he cried. But he kept on going.

Finally, the gang reached the house. They found Lena in a secret passageway.

"The zombies dragged Simone away," Lena told them.

The gang sped through tunnels, dodging zombies as they searched for Simone.

They stepped into the entrance of a cave. It was a strange place, with a large cat statue standing on an altar. Something weird was definitely going on.

"Voodoo," Velma exclaimed.

She turned to Lena, because suddenly Velma guessed the truth. "And Simone wasn't dragged away. When someone is dragged, they leave long heel marks. But I only saw footprints . . . of someone *walking* away!"

Just then a door slid open. "Very clever, Velma," Simone said. She was standing next to a giant moon dial. "But it's too late!"

Simone held up wax dolls of Daphne, Fred, Velma, and Beau. Each doll had a piece of that person's real clothing attached. The pieces had been stolen from the gang's luggage! They were used to make magic voodoo dolls! Velma knew that the dolls could force them to do things they didn't want to do!

Quickly, Simone wound twine around the dolls' arms and legs. The four looked around, wild-eyed. Now they couldn't move!

If the gang could destroy the dolls, the voodoo spell would be broken.

Simone pointed to the moon dial. "At midnight, the ceremony to drain your life forces will begin. Then, Lena and I can live forever!"

"You see," Simone continued, "Lena and I helped settle this island long ago. But then the pirates took over." She nodded toward the cat statue. "We wished for revenge, and we became cat creatures. We can live forever — as long as we have victims."

The zombies! Velma realized. Moonscar and the others had been victims, too. And they were only trying to help, to warn the unsuspecting gang!

The moon dial read midnight now. It was time.
Simone and Lena slinked closer to the foursome.
Suddenly, their clothes tore free — and the
two weird women turned into
hideous cat creatures. Monsters!
   Just then, Captain Jacques —
another cat creature! — chased
Scooby and Shaggy inside the cave.
   "Ooof!" cried Shaggy as he
accidentally kicked the wax dolls.
   Velma strained to reach
them . . . almost . . . almost.
   She had them!

But she had to work quickly. Lena and Simone grabbed Scooby and Shaggy, ready to drain their life force.

Suddenly, the cat creatures were flung against the wall. Daphne and Velma had turned the tables on the evil twosome and changed the voodoo dolls into Lena and Simone dolls!

"Noooo!" howled the monsters as the shadow moved past midnight. Their skin wrinkled and they grew instantly older. Finally, Lena, Simone — and Jacques, too — turned to dust and blew away.

Zombies stumbled forward. "Thank you," one soldier whispered. A gusting wind blew through the cave. The ooze lifted, and the skeletons crumbled to the floor.

"Zoinks!" Shaggy said. "What happened to them?"

Velma smiled. "They can finally rest in peace."

Later, Beau led the gang back to the ferry.

"I'm sorry we suspected you," Velma told him.

Daphne nodded. But she was thinking, too, about her show. They'd actually seen real, live ghosts, but they had no camera. No film — and no proof.

"I've got nothing," she told the others.

"And the police will never buy this story," Velma added.

"Don't be so sure," said Beau, taking out a police badge.

"Detective!" Daphne grinned. "Have you ever been on TV?"